MEAD-HILL

SOUTH PEEVEETOE, TEXAS

~~~

Tommy LeVrier

MEAD-HILL

in
association
with

Jo Ann Tedesco

SOUTH PEEVEETOE, TEXAS
Copyright © 2019 MEAD-HILL

ISBN-10 1695475267
ISBN-13 978-1695475267

Published in the United States and worldwide by MEAD-HILL
www.mead-hill.com
Manufactured in the United States of America

Book Design by Zhou Wenjing, Joseph Janeti

First Edition

CONTENTS

Frankenstein and the Polio Girl … … … … … … … … 3

Oilfield Roosevelt … … … … … … … … … … … … 13

Rupert, Frankie, Rose, and Stubby … … … … … … … 21

Other Version of Prior Story … … … … … … … … … 33

Billy Hole … … … … … … … … … … … … … … … … 37

Fatty's Trip to the Bank … … … … … … … … … … … 47

Terry Dwayne … … … … … … … … … … … … … … … 55

Little Donald Lee Jr. & Sputnik … … … … … … … … 65

Little Piggy's Uncle's Café … … … … … … … … … … 67

Claude Wilkies and his poor white family … … … … 71

South Peeveetoe Vignettes … … … … … … … … … … 75

About the Author

SOUTH PEEVEETOE, TEXAS

a MEAD-HILL WRITER'S VOICE ⊠ publication -
complete, unedited, and exactly
as presented by the author...

FRANKENSTEIN AND THE POLIO GIRL

John Ray pushes his lawn mower and follows the tractor that grades the dirt roads of the "city" of South Peevee-toe, population 1,005. He inhales the slight oily smell of the freshly graded dirt and smiles. John Ray wants to walk barefoot in the soft line of dirt that the tractor pushes to the side of the road but he figures he is too old for that now.

He swigs the last of his 16-ounce Mr. Cola and picks at a back tooth with a toothpick. Part of the brown crumbling tooth sticks to the toothpick and he examines it. His real name is John but he likes for people to call him "Ray," after his father.

John Ray is real proud of his father, although nobody else is. Before his last mowing job of the day, John Ray needs to stop by the gas station where his father works so he can fill-up a large glass bottle with gas. He found distilled water bottles worked best. In addition, he wants to remind his daddy of why this particular day is special and like no other.

John Ray hears a whoop behind him. He groans, and does not have to look behind him back to see who it is. He knows who it is.

"Johnny!" yells his next-door neighbor, Clinton.

Ray knows what he wants. Clinton doesn't need to tell

John Ray that he wants to be paid to help mow yards so that he will have enough money for the revival tent show meeting tonight.

"It's Ray," says John Ray. "I told you two dozen times. It's Ray. Ray! Dang it!"

Clinton walks along beside him being gooder than good so as he will be allowed to help mow.

"You going to the revival tent show meeting tonight?" asks Clinton.

"I wouldn't be mowing these yards if I wasn't," says John Ray.

"So whose yard you going to be mow'n?" asks Clinton.

"Me to know and you to find out," says Ray. "I got to drop by the gas station first. Ray Senior might have forgotten about the Revival meeting tonight. He might have been too hung over this morning to remember."

"What time is it?" asks Clinton.

"Half past a monkey's ass," says Ray.

"You forgot the rest of that saying, didn't you?" says Clinton.

After a long silence, Ray says, "You not going to be able to mow barefoot like that. You know what happened to Skippy Perkinsdale."

"Yeah," says Clinton." "Got his foot caught in the lawn mower and lost two toes. He would have lost another if his mother had not of held one of them on in place all the way to the hospital so they could sew it back on."

"Now they say he can't pitch Little League no more," says Ray. "They say now every time he winds up, he falls straight off the pitcher's mound. Now do you want that to happen to you?"

Clinton steps slowly, letting his bare feet sink into the soft, dark dirt at the edge of the road. He feels the cool earth beneath his toes as he weights the obstacles in his mind. Suddenly, he is off and running for his porch and is back in two seconds with his shoes tied around his neck.

Ray Senior is sitting on the curb at the gas station dressed in his usual khaki work clothes and white undershirt underneath. He isn't wearing a hat and you can see his shiny bald spot at the top of his crew cut, the same style that he wore in the Army.

"Uh oh," says Clinton. "Looks like he just got chewed out by Old Man Thibodeaux. Maybe we better hurry up and get the gas and get out of here."

"Working hard?" asks Ray Jr.

"You see any cars in that driveway?" asks Ray Sr.

Ray Jr. didn't, but he admires the way he says it. Ray Jr. loves Ray Senior's voice, sort of low and gravely. Ray Jr. could listen to his father talk for hours about nothing. The years of whiskey and filter less WWII cigarettes left Ray Senior with such a deeply resonant voice that it makes him appear almost educated.

"You hear any bells ringing?" asks Ray Senior. "They's got to be a car in that carport to be busy."

"I don't see old man Thibodeaux either," says Clinton, trying to make light of it.

Ray Senior holds the glare at Clinton for a long time before taking a drag off a Lucky Strike. "I hate that old man with every fiber of my being," says Ray Senior.

"Well, at least he's taking you back this time," says Ray

Jr.

Now Ray Senior's glare is concentrated on his only son. "Ray Jr., I want you to pick up every piece of paper, trash, leaves, in that yard. Then I want you to clean out that septic tank."

Despite everything, Ray Senior could do no wrong in Ray Jr.'s eyes -- even when Ray Jr. had to skip school and go into work for him when he was too hung over to work. That is, when he could hold a job. Ray Senior shifted back and forth between two gas stations in town and boxing groceries at the grocery store.

"But . . . you forgot about the revival tent show tonight. I'll never get all that done and make it by six."

"You going to the Revival Meeting tonight?" asks Clinton.

"I am," says Ray Senior.

"Do you remember why?" asks Ray Jr.

"I do," says Ray Senior.

About this time, a big old Buick driven by the insurance man pulls up and runs over the hose that rings the gas station bell. Ray Senior's expression changed to cheerful and he began to wipe the insurance man's windshield for him in a humble manner.

Clinton, pushing the lawn mower now, balances the full bottle of gas on the edge of the mower and says, "Remember when your Daddy got caught once sneaking into the football game and got run out for drinking?"

"Yeah," says Ray Jr., who now has decided he wants to be called Ray, Jr. rather than just Ray. "They caught on to his plan to beat the ticket prices."

Since they lived right behind the school, Ray Senior would sit on their back porch listening to the high school game and drink cheap whiskey. Once the first half was over, he could sneak into the stadium for the second half without paying. This gave him extra money for wine and liquor. He could take a flask with him when he went so as he could pour it into his Coke cup acquired at the concession stand.

"That was until old Porky Simmons caught him," says Clinton.

"Yeah, one day, Daddy went in a little too soon. Well, it wasn't exactly too soon, it was that old Porky Simmons, who took the tickets, was still at the ticket booth counting up the money at half time. He saw Daddy sneaking in the front gate and went and got the head football coach . . . and he, the football coach, and the deputy sheriff walked Daddy out of the stadium in front of God and everybody."

Ray Jr. could see the humor in the situation and it didn't affect the way he sees his father.

"I hope he don't do that tonight," says Clinton.

Ray Jr. is silent. He is thinking about the revival tonight. It is hard for him to believe it has been a year since the last one. A year since the preacher with the snakes around his neck told his polio sister to take off her brace and walk. And she did! She walked clean across the tent without a brace before falling into the arms of the evangelist.

Next day she was back to normal and couldn't walk two steps without the brace. It had been a year since then and now Ray's family prayed he could cure her altogether now. This time he will be better and maybe she will walk for good. That is, if they pray hard enough.

"Has he seen you wrecked his car yet?" asks Clinton.

"Not hardly," says Ray Jr.

He didn't get it out of the garage this morning. He figures saying it would not start would be a good cause for him being late for work. I am not going to tell him until Sunday morning when he is too hung over to yell."

Ray Jr. would tolerate Clinton today because he was his best friend and Ray Jr. planned to marry his sister someday. She is a good Pentecostal, would make a good wife, and bear him a son that he could name Ray III in honor of his father.

Ray Jr.'s plan was simple. He would drop out of high school, lie about his age so he could get into the pilot program with the Air Force, and then get his G.E.D. After that he would return and marry Clinton's sister.

Ray lets Clinton mow the entire yard while he reflects on the plan for the evening. He figures he can get that little red-haired boy down the street to pick up all the trash in the yard and rake the leaves for little or nothing. As for the septic tank, Ray Senior would be too hung over tomorrow to yell at him for not doing it.

When Clinton finished mowing, Ray Jr. gave him almost half what he was paid for the yard. This still left Ray Jr. with enough money for another Mr. Cola, a *Three Musketeers* bar, and a little something to put in the offering plate tonight.

Clinton and Ray Jr. get to the revival meeting early and get good seats on the front row. They sit next to Ray

Jr.'s sister, who had polio as a child, and Clinton's sister, who Ray Jr. enjoys sitting next to.

After a long while, the crowd stops clapping and singing gospel tunes like "Old Time Religion," and "Shall we gather at the River," and the preacher starts his sermon. He knows that the crowd is mostly here to see the polio girl walk and he milks the drama for the captive audience for all they are worth.

Ray takes a swig of Mr. Cola and says, "I need to pee but I can't now."

"Why not?" asks Clinton.

"The preacher may make my sister walk and I don't want to miss it," says Ray Jr.

They could see Ray Senior sneak through the tent canvas wall just after the offering was passed. This does not pass without notice and the visiting preacher extends his sermon and adds alcohol to his tirade of sins.

"The evantriloquist is talking about your Daddy," says Clinton.

Ray Jr. doesn't bother to correct his pronunciation. He grimaces visible and says, "Now the preacher is never going to stop talking!"

He really needs to pee now and doesn't appreciate Ray Senior holding things up. He doesn't even care if he is in church when he thinks his thoughts against his Father.

"You shouldn't talk against your Father in church," says Clinton's sister. "It's a sin."

"I don't care," says Ray. "I have to pee Goddamnit!"

"Now you got everybody looking," says Clinton's sister while turning beet red.

Ray Jr. can only squint and try to hold it.

Finally, the preacher stops talking and approaches the front row where the Polio Girl is sitting.

He holds his hand over her head and looks up to the sky. The entire Pentecostal congregation hushes when the preacher starts talking to his Heavenly Father. "In the name of the Holy Spirit," says the visiting preacher man. "Our Lord God Almighty. Will you please anoint your sacred powers? Hallowed be thy name; help this pitiful child with your healing powers."

The preacher closes his eyes and yells, "Take, Take, and Take . . . Take off your brace!"

The preacher's assistants scurry to take off Ray Jr.'s sister's brace and help her to her feet.

"She looks excited and scared," says Clinton.

When she starts to wobble, Ray Jr. puts his hand to her back and holds her up in a way that nobody could tell he is doing it. Clinton and Clinton's sister sit alert in case she falls backwards on to them, since she is not light.

"The meek shall inherit the earth!" yells the preacher. "Anything is possible through the King who rides the humble donkey. Jesus work through me!"

The preacher pauses dramatically then releases his hand from the top of her head. Ray Jr.'s polio sister keeps her eyes closed. She figures the harder she prays, the better her chances.

She begins to tremble but is able to stand mostly through Ray Jr. and Clinton holding her up from behind in a way that no one can see.

The preacher begins to back up.

"Come thee," says the preacher. "Come hither. Walk! Walk with Jesus on the mount!"

Ray's sister with polio begins to walk toward the preacher, shaking but steadfast. The preacher backs further away every time she gets almost to him.

Suddenly here is a loud clanging. Ray Jr. closes his eyes. He didn't have to look. Ray Senior had set his pint whiskey bottle on one of the top rows of the portable stands. It falls from the top and rolls all the way down the steps, making a loud clanging sound as it drops to each level. The bottle finally lands on the final step and then seems to leap on its own and roll in the dirt towards the preacher. The bottle spins several times before coming to rest right before the visiting guest evangelist. The preacher's eyes go wide and he looks at the bottle as if it is the Devil himself.

The whole tent turns to look at Ray Senior who tries to hide behind the stands but cannot.

The trance is broken and Ray Jr.'s polio sister falls on top of the skinny preacher, pinning him to the ground. The crowd gasps, fearing he will be crushed but the preacher doesn't miss a beat and yells, "Give me strength! Give me strength! Arise thee, arise! Cast the sin out of this sinner! Cast out!"

His assistants rush to his aid to lift the heavy polio girl off him but he waves them off and yells in a suffocating voice, "No, no! The Lord will come to us. Jesus Christ our Holy Savior will give us strength. She is a sinner, she is a sinner. This is why she cannot walk!" Take out the poison of sin and let her rise!"

Suddenly, he lifts her off of him easy as pie and rises to

his feet with his Bible still intact in his left hand.

He turns to her and says, "Rise. Rise you ungrateful sinner! Fight the Devil! Fight the unholy Satan!"

The polio sister slowly rises to her feet like a new born deer and stands; however shaky, before the preacher. She watches her legs wobble as the preacher begins to back away again. She sways back and forth to hold herself up but somehow keeps her balance.

"Walk, sinner, walk!" continues the preacher man. He lets go of her hand and steps backward saying, "Walk, walk!"

She slowly inches toward the preacher with the fancy haircut, breathing loudly and sweating profusely.

"Help this poor sheep, says the preacher. "The meek shall inherit the earth! Fight the Devil! Fight the Devil!"

Clinton, Ray, and Clinton's sister all sit open-mouthed and silent while the entire Pentecostal congregation breaks out into a version of "It's good enough for me."

Eyes closed, the preacher repeats, "Walk sinner! . . . Walk!"

Ray's polio sister, who had never known anything but suffering all her life despite her sweet nature, smiles at the preacher like a hopeful child. She continues walking awkwardly in a determined nature toward the preacher, eyes wild, like some sort of Frankenstein.

OILFIELD ROOSEVELT

I SAW SOMETHING TODAY I COULDN'T BELIEVE

Little Piggy lay on the cold, red, cement floor of Mr. Green's Barber Shop reading comic books one afternoon in early August. Various stuffed wild animals Mr. Green had bagged and mounted on the walls - deer, bobcat, and a menacing wild boar with long jagged yellow teeth - seemed to be staring at him. Little Piggy ignored them and went back to reading is copy of the Adventures of Flash.

A retired oilfield worker slumbered in a green wooden chair. He wore what he always wore. Khaki pants, khaki shirt, straw cowboy hat, and work boots bought from the mercantile store in South Peeveetoe. It was owned by a woman who claimed to be a survivor of a German prison camp in World War Two. She had a little tattoo with small numbers written on her wrist. Little Piggy's father was small like Piggy. They wanted to use him as a machine gunner in the bottom of a World War Two bomber, since he was one of the few that fit, but he opted to become a cook instead.

Portervae, a tall, skinny, young man with long skinny Elvis sideburns and a shiny slicked back ducktail sat in the barber chair. He moved a toothpick to the other side of his mouth and reflected out loud.

"I saw something today I couldn't believe." Portavae said.

Mr. Green stepped back, knocked the loose hair off his Shriner tie, and waited with his scissors poised in silence. The barber shop went quiet save the whirling sound of the air conditioner. The stuffed animals seemed to be waiting in earnest for Portervae's reply.

He paused for effect and stared blankly at the wall calendar underneath one of the deer heads with especially big antlers. The calendar detailed the football schedule of the fighting South Peeveetoe Bearcats including their annual homecoming game with their rival, the Karankawa Point Cannibals. Little Piggy reached for an Aquaman comic but stopped in mid-air to hear what Portevae had to say.

"I saw Oilfield Roosevelt working today," he said.

A long, shocked silence was eventually interrupted by the whole shop bursting into laughter. The retired oilfield worker woke up with a loud snort.

Portavae was referring to the local town idiot, or at least one of them, in South Peeveetoe. Oilfield Roosevelt was the butt of many of the town jokes. He was the ne'r-do-well who lived on the outskirts of the oilfields in a one-room shack.

"Doing what?" Mr. Green asked incredulously.

After the laughter died down, Portavae replied in a triumphant manner.

"He was pushing a wheel barrel next door," he said.

"For what," asked the retired oilfield worker.

"For the construction site after the big fire," Portavae

said.

The recent fire they were referring to was huge with large leaping flames throughout downtown South Peeveetoe. They say it was caused by Old Man Buster and his new cafe. Some think the reason he left a coffee pot on the stove on purpose. That he did it so he could collect insurance because he couldn't keep up with the other more established cafes in town. The fire burned down, his cafe, the Five and Dime, and the furniture store. The large brick wall at the drugstore finally caused the fire to stop altogether.

Piggy was particularly glad to see it had not burned down the South Peeveetoe Picture Show as he had seen his first horror movie there *The Creature from the Black Lagoon.*

Just at that very moment, they could see Oilfield Roosevelt push a wheelbarrow filled with rocks just outside the window of the barber shop. The whole room jumped up and ran to the window for the unusual sight of Oilfield Roosevelt pushing a wheel barrel full of rocks. He wore what he always wore, even in summer he could be seen dressed in a heavy wool jacket, a vest, wool pants, and an overcoat slung over his shoulder. Tall and slim, he topped it off with round silver metal round glasses and a shiny silver pocket watch and chain.

Oil Field Roosevelt lived in a shack in the oilfields for as long as anyone could remember. One day, Little Piggy, the mean preacher's boy, and the retarded boy they called Pack rat, picked his homemade lock and went inside to explore his home. They found a cot, a tin cup, some canned food, extra wool sweaters and jackets, and that was about all.

Pack Rat took a keen interest in Oilfield Roosevelt. He badgered him at every turn in the road. Pack rat was much taller and bigger than the other kids around his age. He was sort of like that character in that Steinbeck novel that the kids were forced to read at school. They regarded Pack Rat as normal, however, save a few things. He liked to pull toy trucks attached to a cotton rope. As he pulled them, he made truck sounds as if they were shifting gears or making the loud gushing sound of air brakes as the imaginary trucks stopped.

Other than that, he was fairly normal. Always dressed in khakis, a white T-Shirt, heavy work boots, and a cap from his collection of welding caps, he was fascinated by big trucks and covered the walls of his room with pictures of trucks cut out from truck magazines. The only thing that bothered Piggy about him was that he liked to shoot dogs in the neighborhood, especially Chihuahuas like Sputnik of whom he liked to shoot in the genitals, with his pump pellet rifle.

One day Pack Rat pumped his pellet gun up over and over in preparation of shooting a dog far down at the end of the street. Piggy asked him to stop pumping up the gun so much but he refused. He kept pumping with all his might until he could barely pump it anymore. He took aim at the dog and fired. To their surprise, the dog fell over dead.

They went to investigate the dog and Old Man Dog Man came out of his house. It was one of Old Man Dog Man's numerous dogs. He began to curse Pack Rat and tried to take his pellet rifle away from him. Pack Rat and the grown man wrestled for the gun but, due to his superior size and strength, he could not separate the gun from Pack rat's huge arms.

Another day Pack Rat and the preacher's boy talked Piggy into visiting Roosevelt's shack again. When they got there they found Oilfield Roosevelt standing in the doorway of his proud shack, eating a can of sardines. The three stopped in their tracks. He yelled at Pack Rat and called him, "a little crazy." On this, all three of the invaders took off running lickety split.

Oilfield Roosevelt had some unusual hobbies. He like to hitchhike some 15 miles away to the nearest town so he could watch the men work at a gas station. He preferred this over going to going to the high school football game like everyone else. Watching men work at the gas station in Karankawa Point was his idea of entertainment. He picked that also over the Doris Day, war, and Vincent Price movies down at the picture show.

"They say he is kind of smart," Peeveetoe said.

Good stopped cutting and stared at him.

"He's good at math," Green said. "You could ask him questions on a mathematical nature and he could tell you the answer every time."

"You know something," Mr. Green said. "Oilfield Roosevelt was real rich at one time."

The room looked back in quiet shock.

The retired oilfield worker suddenly came to life.

"Yeah," the retired oilfield worker said. "He inherited a whole bunch of money. He moved into a hotel in Beaumont and lived it up. The women loved him. Then when he spent up all the money the women and the people in the hotel did not want anything to do with him."

Life continued this way for Oilfield Roosevelt for years. He lived in his shack in the oilfields and went up to downtown everyday to watch people walk by and shoot the bull with the retired oilfield workers.

One day years later, Oilfield Roosevelt did an unusual thing. He not only attended church, he went an actual wedding. After the ceremony, full of love and exuberance for the lord, Roosevelt forgot himself and ran up and hugged the bride, just like everyone was. Like he was normal. The woman in white recoiled in horror, not believing that she had actually been hugged by the likes of Oilfield Roosevelt with his smelly Salvation Army surplus clothes.

Even though Oilfield Roosevelt was white, he was immediately run out of town. They abruptly tore down his shack and sent him packing. Piggy later heard he moved to Odessa to live with his sister where he died some years later.

Green walked over to his Camel cigarette razor strap and sharpened his straight razor. He gave Portavae a close shave and then massaged his face with Rose Tonic, and combed his hair with Dixie Hair Oil.

Mr. Green gave Piggy a crew cut, rubbed in some Butch Wax, and walked over to a desk in the corner. Piggy gave him a dollar and the barber with the funny ties opened a drawer where he put away the4 dollar and then gave Piggy a piece of Double Bubble gum – a reward for getting a haircut.

Much later as an adult, Little Piggy chewed some of

this same type of bubble gum and it made him dizzy as all get out. He remembered that he always felt that way after a haircut. He thought back then that maybe it was from reading the comic books too fast so he would not have to go to the drugstore and pay for them. He realized it was not Aquaman or Superboy that made him ill. It was that pink bubble gum that made that made him sick all those years.

RUPERT, FRANKIE ROSE, AND STUBBY

Rupert Palmers eyes Stubby Perkinsdale out his living room window. Stubby woke Rupert up early as he always did at this time with his loud banging from across the road.

"As per usual," Rupert mumbles to himself as he sips a second cup of Seaport. Stubby got this nick-name because, while driving drunk one night, he leaned his arm out the passenger window and another car sideswiped him and left him with only a stub on that side. Now that minnow and mowing yards season was over, Stubby needs a new business so he started smashing and crushing cars. When finished flattening them, he takes the cars over to the wreckage yards in Beaumont. Everyday about this time, Stubby would slam a makeshift cast iron ball down on the cars with as much force as a small G.M.C. truck with a shaky homemade winch could muster.

Rupert works the night shift at the shipyard in Beaumont. He'd been there eighteen years, and worked his way all the way up to night watch welder foreman. Rupert had put up with Stubby Perkinsdale as long as he could remember. Just when he got home and finally tossed and turned into a deep sleep, Stubby would start dropping that cast iron ball.

People know Rupert as a quiet man who never bothers

anybody. He, "minded his own business," as they say in South Peeveetoe. This was somewhat out of the ordinary for South Peeveetoe and they look on him with respect, even though they may not express it to him directly.

Rupert's wife, Frankie Rose, a plump redhead, tip-pee-toes up behind him. She "has gained" lately but still has a sweet childlike face and demeanor.

"Stubby's new enterprise," she said.

"Nigger rig," Rupert said. "He nigger rigs everything. I'm beginning to think he is half nigger his own self."

"Maybe you should try going back on the day shift, Rupert," she said.

Rupert never smiled. Wiry and dark complected, he probably had some Cajun blood deep within him. Maybe a little Indian too for that matter. A lot of Coon Asses had some Black Foot or Crow in them in Louisiana which was the state where Rupert was originally born and reared.

"Too hot and too many damned college kids," said Rupert as he wiped his mouth with the sleeve of his shirt. "Besides, I'd miss the differential. More than a dollar an hour more."

"You'd think we'd be used to it by now," said Frankie Rose. "Maybe we should move somewhere else."

Frankie Rose regretted it as soon as she said it. She should know by now that Rupert is too proud to move and too stubborn to let the likes of Stubby Perkinsdale run him off.

Rupert continues looking out the window. Frankie Rose smiles to herself. Two weeks ago saying the wrong thing would have filled her with all kind of gloom. Now nothing seemed to bother her after her trip to the Beaumont psychiatrist. Not even Stubby's ugly-as-sin junkyard dogs that bark all night at nothing seem to bother her anymore.

She had been depressed for months prior and that is when she started to gain. Both her kids had grown up and moved out of the house. Frankie Rose was even beginning to lose her faith in Christ.

It was OK for Rupert, she thought at the time. He had other things. Everybody did, except for Frankie Rose, or so it seemed to her. Rupert had the men he worked with, his fresh water fishing trips, and duck hunting. He didn't seem to need the Lord in his life.

Sunday was his worship day. He worshiped the TV. That's when the pro football games were on. Lately that hadn't been going well either at least not since the television broke down.

She finally confided her troubles one day to her best friend, Margaret Lynn down the street. Frankie Rose told her that she felt she needed to see a psychiatrist before she had a nervous breakdown. Margaret Lynn just scoffed and waved her hand, "You don't need a psychiatrist," she said. "You're just bored that's all. Now that your kids are all grown!"

Margaret Lynn was different, Frankie Rose thought at the time. She, "was busy," and had the garden club and those trips to see flowers in Memphis and what not and what have you. Frankie didn't have any hobbies to occupy her. Her kids had been her hobbies.

Their oldest boy, Buster, is now nineteen and is quiet

and intense like his father. He's stationed in Germany.

"Did you see the letter from Buster," asked Frankie Rose with her arms crossed behind her back in a cute manner, "He got an army medal for sharpshooting."

"Sharpshooting?" asked Rupert and then acted as if he was not proud as he could be as he picked up the sports page.

Their daughter Patty Ann is not like Rupert at all. In fact, she "was just the opposite." Shrill and opinionated, she had always been more like an adult than a child and was always up on the local gossip. She rode her older brother all the time, even to the point of nick-naming him "ignorance."

Patty Ann had loved the Beatles and played their music night and day and decorated her walls with their .45 records. In fact, she even talked Eugenia, the town beautician into cutting her hair just like Ringo's. It was quiet now without Patty Ann though, now that she recently married someone older than her and moved to Lufkin. She had also quit listening to the Beatles who she felt, "was acting like beatniks."

"It's sure quiet without the Beatles," Frankie Rose said.

"I've had enough of the Beatles," Rupert said while almost smiling.

"He's just that way," Frankie Rose tells Margaret Lynn. "People think he's unhappy but he isn't. Rupert is just a person that doesn't smile a lot."

Frankie Rose decided to make a decision for once in her life on her own and chose to go to the psychiatrist anyway. Maybe he could have some pills for her or something. Anything to stave off a nervous breakdown. It proved to be the right thing for her as it had only taken one session and now she felt entirely better.

"It only took one session," she said. "He told me the same thing Margaret Lynn told me. That I was bored and needed to find other things in my life to replace our kids of whom had now grown up on us."

"Huh?" Rupert asked.

"Oh nothing," she said. "Just talking to myself. You get that way after a while."

She was back to her old self. Frankie Rose now feels that she deserved to be in the garden club like everybody else. She filled her life with other things such as the church and has rediscovered Christ as her holy savior. Besides that, she's patiently awaiting for her someday grand kids.

"Who could ask for more?" she said out loud.

"What?" Rupert asked.

Now that her life was enriched, Frankie Rose felt a need to focus on Rupert who was in a bad way. Now that her cup was running over, she felt she has more than enough to give.

Rupert put down his cup of black Seaport on the window sill and said, "It's time I got to work on that television set. I been planning it long enough. Be a while before I can get back to sleep anyways."

He puts a screwdriver between his teeth and climbs behind the huge R.C.A. Frankie goes into the kitchen and returns with a sponge. She raises his cup, wipes the ring it's made, and carefully places the cup down on a fresh orange, straw coaster.

"Man, we got enough wires back here to electrify an

army," said Rupert.

Rupert unscrews the back of the TV and starts adjusting screws. Frankie Rose observes from the front to see if the picture gets any better or worse.

"Turn your vertical a little...no, the other way," she said. "That's better. Now your horizontal. Now turn your color just a little pinch of snuff."

Rupert glares at her bossy manner.

"Are we getting the squiggly lines or not?" he asked in an irritated voice.

"Yeah, you still getting them but now you lost your color," she said in a serious manner.

Rupert turns the screwdriver with a wince. Suddenly there is a flash and a loud jolt that knocks Rupert against the wall. A loose nail in the wall sticks to the back of his head and he drops the screwdriver.

"Shocked the fire out of me!" yelled Rupert.

He pushes the large R.C.A. like it is an enemy and it falls off the metal TV table and hits the floor.

"Well Rupert, you need next time to turn the TV set off before you go to work on it's interior," Frankie Rose said.

Rupert holds the glare for a long time. Frankie Rose focuses on the dusty top of the black aluminum TV stand and said, "Oh look, I didn't know we still had that."

She hadn't seen the top of the metal table for years. Many of the letters were worn off now but you could still see something written on it about the Alamo. Underneath the Alamo lettering is a large red rose and at the corners are rope lassos. Arthur and Frankie Rose had bought the table on their delayed honeymoon many years ago.

Rupert feels the back of his head. He looks at his hand to see blood from the nail in the wall. He starts to throw his screwdriver then stops himself and drops it into a bright red metal toolbox.

Coinciding with the sound of the dropped screwdriver is another smash from the steel ball across the street that makes both of them jump. Before Frankie can say Jack Robinson, Rupert pushes the screen door open and heads toward Stubby's house. He walks in a long legged gait and waves his right arm wildly as he speaks." Say Perkinsdale, could I ask you to move that truck?" yelled Rupert, something he rarely did ever. "You blocking me. I need to pull out my driveway."

Stubby looks up. With a Pell Mell hanging from his lips, Stubby shakes his head no.

Rupert steps back as if shot and heads back to his house and inside the screen door.

"I can't hardly believe it!" he said to Frankie Rose. "After all I put up with all these years? One request in all these years and he won't come and do it!"

Frankie Rose wrings her hands and says, "Don't let Stubby bother you Rupert. He's not right. You know they kicked him out of the army."

Rupert looks out the screen door to see Stubby staring him down.

"That's it!" said Rupert and disappears into the bedroom and emerges with a .32 caliber pistol. He loads it as he walks back toward Stubby.

Frankie Rose follows him, "very nearly in a hysterical state," as she would tell it later.

"Rupert, what's got into you?" Frankie Rose said. "What are you going to do with that gun?"

She grabs his arm but he flings her away. Frankie Rose drops to her knees and begins to pray.

Stubby told his kids many times how he had taken a Mauser bullet over in Germany and showed them the large scar on his calf to prove it. It's unclear at the time, though, whether he was "showing out" in front of his kids or whether he is just being belligerent. Regardless, he didn't want to look bad in front of his kids, both step kids and real ones, after his telling them about fighting Hitler in Germany and Italy.

Looking up, Stubby's eyes are wide with fear but his kids can't see that from where they are standing. His large body shakes but he won't let go of his grip on the lever that controls the cast iron ball.

Stubby begins flapping his stub like a duck wing, as if he is trying to grab a cigarette from his shirt pocket with the stub. He ends out only sort of scratching under his armpit and making friction noises with the stub.

Rupert continues toward him.

"I said move that truck!" yells Rupert. "You not the only one that fought the Germans!"

In his fidgeting, Stubby accidentally drops the lever and the heavy ball falls on top of the roof of an old Chevy.

Rupert jumps back at the sound, his eyes white against his dark skin. He aims the pistol at Stubby and "bam, bam, bam," went the bullets. The first one hit Stubby in the shoulder just above the stub. The second in the right cheek and then out the other side. Stubby staggers and turns his back on Rupert who tries to unload the rest of the shells into Stubby's back but misses out of nervousness.

Stubby remains standing and turns, hunched over, to face Rupert and says in a low gravely voice, "I'll kill you. I'll kill you."

Rupert fires again but hears only the click of an empty chamber. He drops the gun and begins to cry. No one had ever seen Rupert cry before, save Frankie Rose, and that was only when he lost his mother and also their little weenie dog which they had had for some sixteen years. Frankie pats him and motions for one of Stubby's step sons to get the volunteer ambulance corps.

"It's OK honey, it's all right," said Frankie Rose but her face is puzzled.

Little Donald Lee Jr. who is chubby, short, and blond-headed, runs for his grandma's house as Stubby does not own his own phone.

"I am going to call Sheriff Kranz!" he yells as he runs. He stops running, turns, cups his hands, and yells, "And the ambulance!"

Donald Lee emerges from his grandma's house carrying an automatic shotgun that his daddy had given him for his birthday. His two half brothers, Clark and Odet, both of whom wear coke-bottle-thick glasses, stop him in the backyard before Sheriff Kranz shows up.

Donald Lee Jr. fights them and says, "I got to do something. You got to do something when it's your father!"

He breaks free and runs back to the site of the shooting to find Sheriff Kranz pulling up in his green Buick with the big red siren on the dash.

"I hear the Hearse, I meant the ambulance, coming," says Odet. It's a natural enough mistake as the volunteer ambulance is actually a converted hearse painted white with a large red cross on the door.

The hearse pulls into the driveway and they load Stubby on to the stretcher. Donald Lee Jr. is beside himself and fights to ride with him but Stubby just stares back at him blankly with glazed fish-like eyes.

"You can't go with him Donald Lee," said Clark, taking on a real brother, as opposed to half brother, role for the first time. "They radioed Doc Gibbons to meet them at the crossroads so he can work on him on the way to the hospital and save his life."

"Don't die daddy, don't die daddy" cries Donald Lee Jr. as he pushes by them and runs at Sheriff Kranz, who is pulling out in the Buick. The sheriff has not handcuffed Rupert, as he had known him all his life and wants to save him that indignity. Frankie Rose rides in the back seat with him.

Inside, Frankie and Rupert see Donald Lee Jr.'s face smashing up against the window of the car. He is yelling, "At the least you can do is handcuff him! You lucky they stopped me in the backyard! I'd of filled him full of buck shot!"

Sheriff Kranz drives on slowly down Cedar Lane to Main. Once there, he turns left toward the Trinity County Jail as the whole town looks on. Donald Lee Jr. runs behind the car but can't keep up. Once on Farm Road 1964, Rupert sadly watches the Hearse and the fire truck pass them both trailing smoke with sirens blasting.

The next morning they take the hand cuffed Rupert to the courthouse to meet the judge and Stubby's court-appointed lawyer. Curiously, once he re-gained consciousness, Stubby decided not to file charges for attempted murder against him. The judge let Rupert go after he met bail, agreed to pay all Stubby's medical bills not covered by the V.A, and pay a small fine for firearms possession. The judge also insisted, as part of the agreement, that Rupert move out of that neighborhood and as far away from the likes of Stubby as a moving truck could travel.

Rupert gratefully met all these arrangements and he and Frankie Rose picked out a yellow and white wood house nearly a mile and a half away from Stubby by the Pentecostal church. Frankie and her kids bought a new Zenith for Rupert for going through all this. Rupert set the television in the exact same spot the other one had been in the living room of the old house. Once finally settled in, he and Frankie Rose put away the last box and flop down on the couch.

"Well, Rupert, aren't you going to turn it on?" Frankie Rose asked.

Rupert just sits looking at the blank tube. He fiddles with the new remote gadget. He had never had one before and seems fascinated by it.

"I don't want to turn it on just yet," he said. "It's sort of peaceful just to look at that green, blank screen."

"I just have to say it Rupert," said Frankie Rose. "You seem to be much more happier and more relaxed like now that you finally moved away from Stubby's house."

A slight crinkle next to his left eye indicates that he is

amused although nobody could tell this by sight, save Frankie Rose.

"It's the smartest thing I ever done," Rupert said. "I wished I had done it a long time ago."

OTHER VERSION OF PRIOR STORY

That night at the Catholic Hospital, Donald Lee Jr. cries into the crisp white sheets at the foot of his daddy's bed in the intensive care room. Stubby, hooked up to several machines, snores loudly.

"Don't let him die mama!" cries Donald Lee Jr. It is understandable that Donald Lee Jr. feels this way. He and his sister Maddy LuAnn are Stubby's only kids that aren't step children. He was particularly fond of his only girl and was right in doing so, according to his neighbors, Frankie Rose and Margaret Lynn. They both once told him they always agreed that Maddy LuAnn, with her curly blond hair and blue eyes "was the prettiest baby that they had ever seen."

Clark, for the first time, realizes he is now the oldest and somehow knows just how to act, and says, "It's good Maddy LuAnn wasn't there when Rupert shot him."

Maddy LuAnn was taller now and heavier than she was as a baby and looks more like everyone else in South Peeveetoe. She tries to comfort Donald Lee Jr. by putting her hand on his back. This gets him to finally stop crying.

The mustached surgeon walks in and a nurse with a starched cap gives him the x-rays. He studies them as he walks over to Stubby's family.

"I think he is well enough to transfer him to the V.A."

he said calmly.

The next day with puffy eyes and a voice hoarse from crying, Donald Lee Jr. explains the incident from the back of a pick up truck to anyone who would listen, and there are plenty that will. He didn't mind telling the same story over and over again even though he might change it a little each time he tells it.

"The surgeon said it was his size that saved him," says Donald Lee Jr. "You know, he's a big man. Almost six foot three and nearly three hundred and fifty pounds. Doctor said it would have killed anybody else."

He stuck his fingers inside his mouth as he explains the shooting.

"The first one went through his cheek then down through his upper lip and then up out the back through the other side of the top of his jaw on the other side," he said in a muffled voice. "The second bullet went into his shoulder and they never did get it out. Then daddy turned his back and Mr. Palmers unloaded the rest of the eight shells into his back before he run out of bullets."

Donald Lee hunches over in imitation of his father with his shoulders rounded like a hunchback. He speaks in a raspy voice in imitation of Stubby.

"I'll kill you, I'll kill you," said Donald Lee. "That's was all he said. He was like a graveyard, Halloween zombie or something. I'll kill you, I'll kill you, he kept repeating."

He sits back down on the truck bed and laughs with nervous relief.

"Daddy is used to pain though," he said. "He'd taken bullets before over in Germany. He's still got that big scar on his calf. You know they had big bullets."

"Guess why them, bullets is so high," said a child that is listening. The child hangs out with them in the neighborhood but no one knows his name or who he belongs to. They figure that he is just a relative of somebody who is visiting maybe for the summer.

Clark glares at him and the child looks at the ground.

"I'm tellin' it right, aren't I Clark?" asks Donald Lee Jr. "Just stop me if I'm not." Clark nods for him to go on.

"Oh I'm not mad at Sheriff Kranz for not handcuffing' him," he said. "I could tell he was kind of nervous about it, the way he kept looking in his tear view mirror at Mr. Palmers. In fact, I heard later that Mr. Palmers tried to jump out the speeding car on the way."

Nobody in the crowd knew if this part was actually true or not. They were willing to forgive it, however, along with the eight bullet business as opposed to six, or three, to be more accurate. They could forgive anything since he had almost just lost his daddy. Besides, this was living proof that Christ was real. It was like Jesus himself had reached down and patted little Donald Lee Jr. on his little blond head.

Tearfully Donald Lee Jr. continued, "I went home and got my automatic shot gun. I know I'm just a little kid but you got to do something when it's your father."

"But we stopped him in the backyard," said Clark, interrupting him.

You couldn't tell through his coke bottle thick glasses whether Clark was crying or not. One thing was for sure, he was very proud of Donald Lee Jr. for how he behaved, and himself too, for that matter.

Donald Lee Jr. laughs nervously and said, "Mr. Palmers was coming at him like as if he was in another world. He was so angry he was beside hisself but daddy just stared him down."

Donald Lee Jr.'s voice became very high during this part.

"Daddy just shook his head no and wouldn't back down." he said. "But you know, my daddy didn't even press charges, Mr. Palmers being neighbors and all. That's just the sort of man he is."

Donald Lee Jr. wipes a tear from his eyes with the shoulder of his tee shirt before speaking again.

"I just hope someday that I can be half the man he is."

BILLY HOLE

I n Piggy's view, the bathroom of the old schoolhouse in South Peeveetoe was a joy to take a leak in. It had a red concrete floor, high windows, marble pissers, and wooden booths with names carved in them. Names from the fifties that Piggy just wished he had, like "T.J." or "Jabbo" or "Morry." Piggy could just picture the faces of the names as he would sit taking one. He saw them with black leather jackets with a rabbit's feet hanging from their zippers, cigarettes dangling from their mouths, and their arms around their favorite girl as they drive their convertible street rods down the streets of the city of South Peeveetoe.

Piggy enters this sanctuary on the first day of school, his new crisp, rolled-up blue jeans making squashing sounds as he walks. He pushes open the green swinging door after the end of the first class and is met immediately by a beady-eyed little runt named Adrian wearing a tucked-in plaid shirt. Adrian, known as "the little fart monkey boy," because of his big eyes and quick movements pulls at Piggy as he struggles to escape the bathroom. The look on the little fart monkey boy's face could only be described as terror.

"Hey, what are you doing, you little fart!" said Piggy.

"Billy Hole's in here!" he shouts and struggles past Piggy

out the door for fresh air.

Piggy proceeds forward anyway, not fully comprehending what the little fart monkey boy is talking about.

That's when the fumes hit him.

"God, Billy Hole IS in here!" shouted Piggy.

Other students follow suit and scramble behind the little fart monkey boy to get out of "the boy's lavoratory," as it was politely called.

"Somebody get some gas masks!" yelled Piggy.

The front door swings open and two of the toughest guys in the school enter. Basil Goodson, who looks a good five years older and already has hair on his chest, struts in. He is followed by his sidekick Cat Daddy Nugget.

Nugget is a feisty loud mouth and uses Goodson as protection. Goodson has well earned his reputation as the school bully. His idea of a good time is to fill toe sacks full of empty beer cans and then cruise by nigger town at ninety miles an hour. When he sees one of them walking along the road, he heaves the heavy toe sacks at them out the window, hitting them directly in the chest and yelling, "chocolate drops!"

Once he and Cat Daddy took Percy Wayne Taylor and held him by his ankles out the third floor. Another time, Clyde Meacum, with the goofy face (the one that would sell his wife for a dollar) was trying to take a crap in an outhouse at the auto repair shop across from Goodson's house. Goodson got his daddy's pick-up truck and pulled up and blocked the door of the john so he couldn't get out. He rocked the outdoor shit house back and forth with the truck until everything in it was all over poor old, screaming, afflicted, Clyde Meacum.

Sometimes Goodson and Cat Daddy would taunt the blind man who ran the grocery store. They would throw quarters from across the street near him to see if he would pick them up. When he did, which he always did, they would yell,

"See I told you he wasn't blind!" yelled Goodson.

Cat Daddy picks Piggy up by the collar of his sleeveless tee shirt and said, "What' you doing here, Piggy?"

"Billy Hole's in here," said Piggy.

Cat Daddy drops him and he and Goodson solemnly head for the urinals. Piggy washes his hands and tries to stretch out his shirt before class starts. Deadpan, the other two stand staring blankly at the wall while pissing. This is a silent show of strength that they could take the smell like men. They finish up, shake off, flush, zip up, and step away from the urinals.

Cat Daddy can't take the fumes any longer. He slams his fist as hard as he can into the brick wall, echoing a loud thud throughout.

A rustle can be heard within the stall. It's Billy Hole reading a copy of *Argosy Magazine*. He is absorbed in an article about scuba divers wrestling five-foot gar fish in a lake in Louisiana. The cover of the magazine shows a color photo of a terrified diver who is hanging on to a huge gar fish for dear life.

"These prehistoric gar have huge teeth like razors...," Billy Hole reads out loud.

"What you say Billy Hole?" yelled Goodson.

Billy Hole continues mouthing the words as he reads

but not loud enough for them to hear him.

"Who died in there Billy Hole?" asked Cat daddy.

"Aw shut up," comes a muffled voice from the booth as Billy Hole turns the page of the *Argosy* article.

"Why y'all pick on Billy Hole so bad?" Piggy asked sadly.

Piggy meant it at the time but it was probably a mistake to say it. Billy Hole's real name is actually Billy Joe but no one calls him that. It seems to Piggy that Billy Hole got the blame for everything. His whole family does. Most say it is because he is ugly. Billy Hole actually wasn't all that ugly, save some rather wide nostrils, and Piggy feels there are many uglier than him in the school.

The head football coach says it is because Billy Hole stinks and that the school hall has to spread out when he walks down the middle of it. Billy Hole, and others, inspired the coach to have "smell contests" on some Mondays in the first period P.E. class of which Billy Hole is a member.

In these, "pop quizzes," the coach would line the students up and have them march to the coach, one by one, so he can sniff them. If you failed the sniff test, you went to one group. If you passed, you were let go to go play touch football in the stinging grass. The failed group would have to do sit ups or run laps as punishment. Billy Hole would always fail, however, no matter how much Right Guard he sprayed on before the class.

Billy Holes's sister, Benita Lu, is treated as badly as him, if not worse. Likewise she isn't particularly homely either, thinks Piggy, save the same wide nostrils and a small mole on her cheek. Her so-called ugliness, however, is brought up on a constant basis. Students would chant, "Nah nah Benita Lu, nah nah Benita Lu," whenever they got into an argument with someone over anything.

Piggy figures people pick on them because they are poor white trash. So poor that they had to use an out house out back of their house and a number three wash tub to take a bath in. Maybe it was because of their shiftless father who, "hurt his back in the oil field," and wouldn't work.

"Which one you think is uglier Benita Lu or Billy Hole?" said Goodson.

"I think Benita Lu's uglier than Billy Hole," said Cat Daddy.

"Ain't dog done it!" said Goodson in Billy Hole's direction. "Billy Hole's a lot uglier than Benita Lu!"

"Nah, Nah, Benita Lu's...," said Cat Daddy.

"Don't strike a match Billy Hole, you'll blow us all to the Enco Plant and back!" yelled Goodson.

Piggy decides to try and impress the two toughs so they will like him and not "do the Dutch rub" on his crew-cut head or thump his ears on cold winter mornings. He climbs to the top of Billy Hole's stall and looks down at him.

"Billy Hole, Billy Hole," Piggy chants softly to Billy Hole.

"Get out of here!" said Billy Hole, "I'm trying to read."

Piggy snickers and slides back down. Unfortunately, he slides down right into the arms of Goodson and Cat Daddy who hoist him back up to the top of the booth. They hold on to Piggy's ankles and drop him over the top of the booth and down inside the stall toward Billy Hole.

Billy Hole is too busy reading to notice. He senses something, however, and looks up to see Piggy's round face looking right into his. The two outside continue to lower until Piggy's face is at the level of Billy Hole's feet.

"What in the hell?" asked Billy Hole.

Billy Hole begins to kick Piggy in the head with his brand new size twelve black, pointy-toed shoes from Kress's in Beaumont. He can't reach him though because his pants are hanging around his ankles. He can only kick a short distance like someone trying to crush a roach.

"Pull me up, pull me up!" screamed Piggy.

"Get out of here!" yelled Billy Hole as he hits him with the rolled up magazine.

"I can't," Piggy yelled back.

The two slowly hoist Piggy back up. Billy Hole throws the magazine at him and the pages fan out like a peacock. They drop Piggy on the cement floor and Cat Daddy chases Piggy out the swinging front door, making barking noises like a rabid dog.

Goodson begins rocking the booth. Billy Hole braces himself by putting his hands on the booth walls.

"Hey, what are you doing?" yelled Billy Hole.

Cat Daddy returns with an armful of toilet paper and a spray can of Pine Sol deodorizer. As Goodson continues to rock the booth, Cat Daddy unwraps the paper and throws rolls one by one over the top of the booth. They unfurl and land on Billy Hole's head.

"What in the hell?" asked Billy Hole.

Goodman sprays Pine Sol underneath the booth, causing Billy Hole to have coughing fits like those World War

One soldiers he had read about in the trenches of Europe. He reaches for the latch to get out.

Cat Daddy braces the door of the booth shut. He is trapped. He tries to climb over the top of the booth but is met with a spray from the Pine Sol directly in the face. Billy Hole falls back and tries to crawl underneath the booth but is met by more spray. Blinded, he falls back on the commode rubbing his eyes and screaming, "My eyes, my eyes!"

Meanwhile, Goodson climbs on top of the ledge and jumps out one of the huge windows, only to return with a large water hose. Cat Daddy helps him slide the hose through the window and then Goodson turns on the hose from the outside. Water begins to trickle out as Cat Daddy slides the hose slowly under the booth next to Billy Hole's feet.

He can't see it because he is blinded. Besides, his new shoes are so thick and stiff he can't feel the water anyway. The water gets deeper and deeper as Goodson pulls more length of the hose into the washroom. When Billy Hole's eyes finally clear he can see he is in two inches of water! Wet toilet paper floats at his ankles.

A loud ring reverberates from the building so loudly that chipped paint actually falls off the ceiling.

It's the bell ringing for classes to start.

"Hey, I can't be late on the first day of school!" yelled Billy Hole.

Piggy sticks his head in the bathroom and yells, "Mr. Davison is coming!"

Goodson and Cat Daddy scramble for the door. Billy

Hole smiles to himself, flushes, and rises to open the booth door. Suddenly the lights are shut out and there is a strange hissing sound.

"Cherry Bomb!" yells Goodson as he slams the door.

The cherry bomb zings over Billy Hole's head and lands in the toilet.

Billy Hole turns around to see the cherry bomb sizzling out and says with relief, "Ha, ha, it went out."

"Boom!" There is a tremendous explosion as water and wet toilet paper spurt into Billy Hole's face. The impact knocks him against the booth door, causing the door to break off its hinges. He lands on his back on the door which is now floating in the water. It slides across the room with the near unconscious Billy Hole lying on top of it.

"Look out for the snake Billy Hole!" yelled Cat Daddy.

Goodson has increased the flow of the water from the outside, causing the hose to rise up like a Cobra and head toward Billy Hole. It stops at Billy Hole and sends water cascading over his face. Billy Hole opens his eyes, spits out wet toilet paper, and pushes the hose away.

His magazine floats up next to him and bumps next to his head. It has opened to a girlie picture in the middle of the magazine with a picture of a woman with large breasts clad only in a tiger-striped bikini.

Billy Hole senses someone looming over him. He opens his eyes to see, "B.A.D" Bob Arnold Davison, the high school principal, tall, thin, in a black suit and narrow tie, staring down at him with wild, unbelieving eyes.

He motions with his first finger for Billy Hole to follow him and says, "I need to see you in the office."

Billy Hole sheepishly follows B.A.D. down the hall, his shoes squeaking as he walks. His shoes leave blue-black footprints in their wake.

Piggy sticks his head out of a classroom and says in a high voice, "Good luck Billy Hole!"

B.A.D. stops and stares sternly at Piggy.

Billy yells at Piggy, "You could have said something in my behalf, you little yellow gizzard!"

Some five minutes later, the classes are interrupted by five slow loud licks from B.A.D's paddle. The wet pants cause a sort of muffled splashy sound as the licks echo, one by one, painfully down the hall.

Inside a classroom Goodson, sitting next to Cat Daddy says, "Oh don't mind that. It's just Billy Hole getting paddled again."

After class, all the boys line up to look at Billy Hole who has lowered his pants to reveal the red imprint of B.A.D's paddle on his naked buttocks.

"There is one thing you can say about Billy Hole," said Little Piggy. "He can sure take a beating."

Fatty's Trip to the Bank

Fatty enjoys "his retirement," but that does not mean that he doesn't have errands to run. He's got it down, however, to a usual daily routine. One that allows him to see "his stories" at night on TV and do his art "paintin'" in the afternoon.

First there is the Post Office, then to the store for a loaf of light bread, sweet milk, yard eggs, or what have you, then on to the bank if he should need to go there. Today is a bank day and he sure regrets it. He'll have to drive a good three miles to get to it and there are many he may have to run into along the way.

He stops first at the P.O. There he'll hear all of it. All the latest. Not that it doesn't interest him, of course it does, he won't lie about it. Today, however, he needs to get back to work on a painting. He is working on a portrait of Jesus hanging on the cross with Judas, who betrayed him, at his feet. The sky is particularly difficult with its light blue sky up against white, fluffy clouds which are hard to paint.

Fatty doesn't hold anything against the Jews because of this. In fact, he fought in the bombers in World War Two in order to rescue the Jews from the spell of Hitler. He learned his painting craft there by painting naked girls or devils dropping bombs on the outside of the planes. Fatty picked up many art books in London at the time as they were real cheap then.

His oil painting and charcoal sketches were his religion. His garage studio was his church. Now, finally, since retirement, everyday was Sunday for Fatty. Or, so he had hoped for himself when he retired.

He's on a tight schedule today. After errands, he will have time to paint and mow. After he eats, he can watch his stories on TV tonight. Or so he hopes. That is if it all goes according to plan...

First he runs into Nita, Donald Lee Jr.'s mother, who has lived next to him for quite some time, at the grocery store.

"I'm sorry I hadn't been by to clean your house for you Mr. Fatty but my family has had their troubles again," she said. "My daughter run off with the Pentecostal preacher."

"I thought his wife run off with another woman," Fatty said.

"That was before Mr. Fatty," she said. "That is true. But this time it is him that is doing the running off."

"Didn't they catch your daughter and the preacher having carnal relations in the church pews?" asks Fatty.

Nita looks at the ground. Fatty regrets it as soon as he says it. He should never have brought it up. .

"Well, I got to go check this mail and get back," said Nita.

"Come clean when you can," said Fatty.

Fatty pushes the metal cart around the store, hoping to get out as soon as he can.

"They see you talkin' to yourself Fatty, they liable to take you off in one of them rubber suits," said someone loudly.

Fatty knew who it was immediately by the loud peculiar laugh of Bert. He laughs so loud that the whole store turns and looks at them both.

Bert had worked for Fatty for many years before being lured away by that pesky Godfellens fellow and his oil field rig outfit. It had taken Fatty a long time to get over this fact. He had to get over it, however, as Godfellens now owns the bank and Fatty is forced to deal with him from time to time. Today is one of them days, a fact that he sure regrets.

"Tell me Fatty, is these peaches in season?" Herk asks as he shows Fatty a half-gallon of Peach ice cream.

"I don't know," said Fatty.

"The doctor says I need to only eat fresh and nothing with, oh, I forget now what he called them," said Bert.

"It wasn't salt was it?" Fatty asked.

"No, it's something else," Herk says.

The store is easy enough and Fatty begins the long drive to the bank. He sure hopes old man Godfellen and his son Junior are out.

First traffic is slowed as old Jesse Hargett is hauling trash to the dump in his horse-driven wagon and is blocking the road. Three dirty little kids are riding in the back of the wagon, much to Jesse's chagrin. Fatty slows until he can hear the clippity clop of the horse hoofs on the pavement. Fatty has to wait until the other lane is clear until he can pass. Fatty makes a point to wave to Charlie as he passes him.

"At least he's willing to work for a living, unlike some

others, despite a steel plate in his head from the war," Fatty said to himself. "I just wish there was more just like him."

There is a dead dog in the road that someone has run over. Fatty honks his horn to scare away the feasting vultures.

"Must have been some little boy's pet," said Mrs Fatty to him.

Fatty hears the voice clean as day then realizes it is his wife's voice and she has been long dead.

"She was sure kind," said Fatty with a slight tear in his eye. "She always took good care of me and my boys."

Fatty is snapped out of his reverie as he has to slam on the brakes to not hit the object in front of him. At first he can't make head nor tail of it and has to squint. All he can see are bright orange flags.

"Construction on the highway again?" he said to himself. "They always working this road. Seems like the government has to look for ways to waste tax money. This road don't even need paving. Aw hell, what can you do?"

Fatty comes to another stop. He could see more clearly now. It isn't construction, it's just Connie Payne on her bicycle. She has attached bright orange flags with long poles to each side of the bike so cars can see her. The bike and the flags are taking up the whole lane.

Connie is pedaling as slow as possible and holds up a whole line of cars and trucks behind her. The left lane slows down to see what is holding everyone up. They shake their heads in dismay and look at Fatty as they pass.

Fatty jumps as he hears a snorting sound. Jesse Hargett has caught up with him and he is passing him on the right shoulder, his horse dropping you-know-what as it goes by. Fatty understands though and knows she "is special" and doesn't know any better. She is the daughter of the mayor and his wife and you cannot blame her for her behavior as both of her parents, "weren't right."

Her father had tried to get rich off of South Peeveetoe by coming up with a grand scheme to make it incorporated into a city, despite less than two thousand people in it. Fatty and some others knew better. He was only trying to get those government contracts to pave the streets so he could skim off the top and end up rich. Or so he thought.

They elected him anyway and South Peeveetoe got incorporated "as a city," because of it. It only made things worse and cut them out from state assistance that they could have got if they had not been a city. The streets never did get paved and they only had grated roads with an oil coating over it which didn't do much but raise dust. The mayor didn't get rich off it like he hoped and had to stay working running his Conoco gas and oil station.

His wife was even worse than the mayor. She was like a little old lady who dressed and acted much older than her age. It was his daughter, Connie, the one on the bicycle, in question now, who bore the brunt of this family. The mayor's son was lucky as the judge gave him a choice of the Marines or prison for stealing parts to put on his street rod. The Marines turned out to be the best thing for him.

Her mother dressed Connie exactly in the manner that she herself dressed. Clad in long skirts, brown sweaters, and round glasses, Connie ended up so nervous-acting that they ended up keeping her behind in the special education class.

"She always dressed Connie like a little old lady," he heard his wife say. "And didn't teach her anything but how to crochet and mow yards. How are you supposed to make a living doing that?

"Kids are too good now to mow yards for money," Fatty said to his wife.

The delay is OK, though as it gives Fatty a time to take in a little scenery. He could forget about his schedule for a moment and enjoy the quiet. Fatty watches a nutria swim downstream, snapping turtles leap from rusty pipes into the muddy water, and a hawk glide silently overhead as he waits for the traffic in the next lane to clear.

Fatty is finally able to pass but he is slowed again in less than three-fourths of a mile.

"Aw hell," said Fatty, "A passing train."

The cross roads close before him. Red lights flash and loud clanging bells signal a train coming. Fatty puts his fingers in both ears. A hobo waves at Fatty. He waves back before catching himself.

When the noise of the grimy yellow freight cars finally begin to subside, Fatty unstuffs his ears and looks behind him to see a whole line of people behind him at the light. Connie Payne, Jesse Hargett, and the dirty little boys in the back of the wagon wait patiently for the train to pass.

Fatty wants to throw up his hands and said to himself, "How is it that you work hard for something and they don't do nothing and you both end up in the same place?"

Fatty knew better. No one had an answer for that one. All Fatty knew was that he would never get to the bank before two. "Aw shoot," said Fatty. "I'm never going to get any paintin' done at this rate."

The long train finally passes and Fatty carefully pulls into the bank parking lot. He gets out of the car and heads for the front door. Just as he arrives the bank door slams in his face and a cardboard sign that reads, "closed," swings back and forth before him.

Fatty sighs heavily and looks at the ground.

"Shoot," he said out loud to himself. "If I'm ever going to get anything done, I'm going to have to let go of some of this other old stuff!"

TERRY DWAYNE

Terry Dwayne Thornton was skinny with blond, stringy hair that constantly fell in his face, cloudy blue eyes, and always wore cowboy shirts with pearl buttons. Little Piggy always thought that Terry Dwayne's head was far too big for the rest of his body.

Little Piggy and his gang called him "Terry Dwayne Raisin' Cane," because of an unfortunate remark that Thornton once made to them. While standing under the big pecan tree on the far side of the school yard, Terry Dwayne ran up to them in a full gallop. His eyes wild, head held back, he yelled. "Fight, fight, somebody's raisin' cane over there, somebody's raisin' cane!"

The reference was to a fight between two girls, something that didn't happen that often at South Peeveetoe High. It was not to be missed, but Piggy feigned apathy. Piggy's gang was tar more fascinated by what he just said than the fight, which would probably be over by the time they got there. Besides, girls couldn't right. All it would be probably was some harmless hair pulling between two sissies. From then on Piggy and his buddies tormented Poor Terry Dwayne with his new nickname.

"Here come Terry Dwayne Raisin' Cane, here come Terry Dwayne Raisin' Cane," they would yell every time they saw him.

Not that he didn't ask for it, thought Piggy. He was just one of those hard luck guys. Sort of "stewpid." Like the way he acted on the yellow school bus. Terry Dwayne picked fights everyday with the fattest guy on the bus. He never seemed to learn. Of course, the big tat bully was too dumb to realize that it was just Terry Dwayne's way of trying to be friends with him. He was trying to impress him but he was going about it the wrong way.

Thornton would trade punches with this guy, Basil (pronounced "Base ill" in South Peeveetoe) on a daily basis on the way to class. Basil was not only a bully and older than him, he was also the former catcher on the Little League team. He couldn't continue playing in high school though because South Peeveetoe wasn't big enough to have a baseball team. And besides, people there thought that anything but football was sissy stuff. They got a big charge out of it when the new Methodist preacher's boy cried when he found out that there was no high school baseball team in South Peeve.

Terry Dwayne Thornton would be in tears every day before the first class started from trading licks with the big fat bully. Kids of all ages were loaded on this bus as Old Man Granger picked them up as far north as the farms on the prairie and as far east as the graveyard. One day, however, these fights finally came to a climax and Piggy just happened to be there.

Basil was in a particularly sadistic mood this day as he sat in a vinyl brown seat that was meant for three. He stretched his black-pointed toe leather shoes out over the end of the seat and leaned one arm each over the rusty iron metal bars over the seats, revealing his sweaty arm pits. He straightened his dark brown short-sleeved shirt, that seemed to bring out his numerous freckles even more, and raised his white sleeveless undershirt underneath it, to stick his nose down there to see it he smelled OK.

"What you smellin,' Basil?" asked Thornton in a high squeaky voice. "Your upper lip?"

Basil glared at him. He had a right to be sensitive. No matter how much Right Guard and Old Spice Basil put on, he always looked and smelled oily, like the pigs his daddy raised. The little white powdery smudges of Clearasil on his chin only made it worse.

Basil brushed back his coal-black hair, glared at him and said, "Wanna trade licks today Thorn Ass?"

"It's Thornton, not Thorn Ass," said Terry Dwayne. "Terry Dwayne to you."

Basil clapped his hands, slid to edge of the seat, and said, "Come on Thorn ass hit me, I dare you."

With that, he rolled up his sleeve as far as his big fat arms would let him and then closed his eyes in exaggerated fear. This action revealed a tattoo, pink and faded blue of something that looked like a mermaid with an anchor above it.

Thornton was obviously impressed, but tried to hide it. Piggy knew where he got the tattoo. He had heard Basil brag one day that he had got it one summer while working with his brother in Houston on a tug boat.

"Where'd you get the tattoo?" asked Terry Dwayne. "I ain't never seen it before."

Piggy could see that he was just now trying to be

friends with the big fat bully but Basil wasn't smart enough to see it. Maybe he just liked being the biggest guy in the bus. It was a rare distinction as the other buses had bigger kids than Basil. Besides, Piggy also figured that it was better that he picked on Thornton than on Little Piggy.

Basil didn't reply to him. He covered his left nostril with one hand and blew a stream of watery, white snot from his other nostril on to Terry Dwayne's western shirt. Thornton looked up with mock horror and anger.

Piggy knew this was fake as he knew that Dwayne didn't really care about the snot so much, but knew he had to show he was angry as to save face with the other kids. Basil was not only the fattest but the oldest guy on the bus. He was nearly nineteen and still not graduated. He lived out on a small farm on prairie near the cemetery and was always the last one on the bus at the end of the day. Nobody knew anything about his Parents. Piggy knew though that he did have one younger sister who was even uglier then him but not nearly as tat. She did, however, wear braces like Basil did and had just as many freckles.

Basil sat up straight and looked at Terry Dwayne, eyes wide, like an ape. Thornton didn't know how to stop the everyday ritual at this point as per usual. He had gotten it started and now trading licks with Basil had become an avalanche that he couldn't stop.

"I don't see how you can afford braces being as your daddy's a dirt farmer," said Terry Dwayne.

Basil hauled off and popped Thornton on the shoulder with a huge fist. Terry Dwayne flinched from the blow and his eves went watery.

"It didn't hurt," said Thornton.

"The hell you say Thorn Ass," said Basil. "Why you cryin' then? Hey, look everybody! Thorn Ass is cryin' like a little titty baby!"

Terry Dwayne knew he had to respond to the challenge at this point or everyone would be laughing at him or so he thought in his own mind. Piggy thought it might be just the opposite. Terry Dwayne rolled to the edge of the seat and swung with all his might, putting all his not too considerable weight behind it. It made a loud popping sound but did little damage.

"The misquotes is shore terrible out here," said Basil.

Piggy led the chorus of the younger kids in laughter at the remark.

Terry Dwayne's second cousin, Winston Rayland Robinson, was there, sitting coolly in a seat to himself, shirt unbuttoned, and smelling of Brut. He wouldn't help his cousin despite being tall for his age and having a much better chance against Basil. And Basil knew it. Still, he didn't help him. Winston felt it would make him look not cool. Especially since this was Friday. Friday was Pep Rally day and Winston Rayland was wearing his new red blazer.

Winston Rayland just sat, legs outstretched, taking up a whole seat to himself, and crunched on shaved ice from a cherry coke from The Stump, a malt shop in South Peeveetoe made out of cement and shaped and painted to look like a tree stump. Besides from the blazer, a fight would muss Winston Rayland's duck tail hair style or crease his brown and green plaid slacks.

He and Terry Dwayne weren't really cousins, anyway.

They just called themselves that as both at their parents drank with each other. Because of that, the two were always seen together, especially at the drive-in movie where their parents would drop them so as they could go to the white beer joints.

Winston Rayland had once confided to Piggy that, "Terry Dwayne's parents don't care about him and nobody wants him. That's why he started smoking cigarettes." This made Piggy feel sort of good, not so much that he felt sorry for Terry Dwayne, but that he was proud that someone of Winston Rayland's age and stature had confided in him.

Basil pointed his short fat finger at him again, "You cryin' Thornton. You cryin.' Look at sissy thorn ass!"

"You done failed twice," said Terry Dwayne. "You ought to be in the National Guard like everybody else your age."

Bam! Basil popped Terry Dwayne on the arm with tremendous force.

"Have mercy on Percy!" said Piggy. "Don't give Terry Dwayne no pain!"

Piggy thought he was safe with this remark. He figured he could side with Basil due to Piggy's "friendship" with Winston Rayland and Basil wouldn't attack him too.

Basil snorted like a donkey and looked back at the grinning elementary kids on the bus.

"Aw shut up," Terry Dwayne said to Piggy.

Basil raises the shirt sleeve at his other arm and said, "Go ahead Thorn Ass, hit me, you can't hurt me, at least not with them little skinny girl taps you got."

He responded with still another blow that just bounced off Basil's big tat arm.

Basil retaliated with a thudding swing that sent Terry Dwayne sliding across the vinyl seat and up against the metal school bus wall. His head slammed against a small nail that was sticking out there and he gasped in pain.

"Hey man," said Piggy, "I hate to tell you this but your head's bleeding."

Terry Dwayne felt his scalp, checked his hand, and saw blood. He laughed in a pale voice.

Basil held up a fist with his middle knuckle protruding. "I'll frog you Ass Thorn," said Basil.

He struck Terry Dwayne on the thigh as hard as he could with the knuckle that was sticking out. Thornton grasped his leg and went double, causing his scalp to bleed all over the worn metal bus floor.

One of the little kids yelled to the bus driver.

"Shut up," yelled Basil to the frightened child who then ran to the back of the bus and tried to unlock the emergency back door or the bus.

"Thorn Ass ain't gonna do nuthin," said Piggy, knowing they were almost to school now and he would be sate. "Terry Dwayne Raisin' Cane won't raise no cane."

"You don't worry about it you little fatty," said Terry Dwayne tearfully to Piggy.

Basil held his eyes wide, leaned forward to taunt his victim and said, "What you going to do about it Raisin' Thorn Ass."

Terry Dwayne paused then saw his chance. He saw an out. "Monkey vomit, camel snot, Terry Dwayne Raisin' Cane Thorn Ass put him on the top!" said Piggy.

Basil stuck his hand in Thornton's Lace. Terry Dwayne

then threw his books at Basil and then, instead of jumping on top of him, leaped for Piggy. He knocked Piggy down on the dirty floor and the two of them struggled for a choke hold as the other kids cheered them on. You could hear the buttons snap off Terry Dwayne's western shirt as the two rolled on the floor.

Old man Granger, the bus driver with the brown Protruding teeth, dressed in khaki pants and shirts, walked to the back of the bus, pushing kids aside. With a filter less Lucky Strike dangling from his lips, he managed to break up the two. Basil, meanwhile, slipped behind the bus driver, and sneaked oft the bus. He didn't want to be late for the first class and did not get beat for being in a fight. The rest of the kids ran off the bus too.

Ole man Granger helped Piggy and Terry Dwayne up. They were all black from the smudge on the floor. Piggy ran down the bus aisle and Terry Dwayne followed him with Granger close behind.

"I toll 'em to stop, I toll 'em to stop," said Granger to himself out loud.

When Terry Dwayne finally stumbled down the bus steps, Basil was there to trip him, causing Thornton to tall on his face in the gravel.

"Say Thorn Ass, you better hurry up, you late, Mid dah Dell Dell gonna beat you with his board," said Basil.

There was then the loud shrill sound of the first bell. He had five minutes to get to his locker and get to class before the second bell went off.

Terry Dwayne slowly lifted his head. Little bits of white shell and gravel stuck to his face.

He glared at Basil and yelled, "I'm gonna oyster fish this summer down at the bay and I'm going to buy me that red Cadillac convertible with the white interior and then I'm gonna come back and show y'all all up."

"Then what?" yelled Basil.

"I'm going to drive it off a cliff," said Terry Dwayne.

"Where you going to find a cliff in East Texas?" yelled Basil with a sadistic grin.

Terry Dwayne's face then fell back into the gravel as the second bell went off.

"Hey Thorn Ass!" yelled Basil. "You already late!"

LITTLE DONALD LEE JR. AND SPUTNIK

Little Donald Lee Jr. could hear them whispering in the kitchen. He could tell by the way his mama and his oldest step-brother Clark were talking that something was wrong.

"Mr. Perkensdale, I'm still calling him that, I meant, your step grandpa...we just got the call," said Nita. "Donald Lee Jr's real grandpa, your step granddaddy, is at the morgue drawer, I meant, the hospital."

"Why?" asked Clark, his eyes already starting to well behind his coke-bottle-thick glasses.

"They say Mr. Perkensdale was coming home from the white beer joint and his dark blue Pontiac skidded at the curve," she said. He went through the bridge and into the creek where he was killed instantly."

Donald Lee listens with one ear. His grandpa was dead but somehow it doesn't seem real. His grandpa and his dog, Sputnik, a Chihuahua that he took everywhere with him, could not be gone.

"I don't know how Donald Lee Jr.'s ever going to take it," said Nita. "You know there is only two of y'all that was his real grand kids. And he is one of 'em."

"He sure probably will take it hard," said Clark.

"They was awful close," said Nita.

"Used to take Donald Lee Jr. with him to the beer joint

and let him sit on a bar stool with him," says Clark. "Mr. Perkensdale gave Donald Lee Jr. all the Sugar Babies and Cokes and them little yeller peanut butter crackers he could eat."

"I remember," said Nita. "Mr. Perkensdale used to put Sputnik on the bar and let him drink out of his Falstaff glass. Them ones in the bar thought it was the funniest thing in the world. Donald Lee Jr. liked to watch him sprinkle salt into his beer and make it foam up. When the dog drank, he would look up with that foam on his mouth and it looked like he had rabies. He then had him walk down the bar and he would walk like he was drunk as all get out."

They both suddenly feel a presence. Nita and Clark look up to see little Donald Lee Jr. standing in the doorway in his flannel bathrobe, his yellow pajamas with the horse-shoes on them, and his little house shoes.

Neither knows exactly what to say. They aren't sure how Donald Lee Jr. will take the news.

In a calm voice that doesn't fit the situation, Donald Lee Jr. said, "Did they ever find Sputnik?"

"No," said Clark softly. "He probably floated down the creek somewhere."

LITTLE PIGGY'S UNCLE'S CAFE

Piggy's uncle almost never got riled about anything, especially in front of his mother, who everyone knows as "Granny." When he does get angry, which isn't often, he makes these loud hissing sounds like a locust. Today is one of those days for hissing.

On his way back from the hardware store with granny, he passes Old Man Mitchell out plowing in his side yard. He quickly rounds the curve at the Methodist church and heads back. Piggy's uncle needs to have another look.

After all, wasn't it Mitchell that was very nearly driving him out of business? He pulls up slowly and comes to a stop on the other side of the road of Mitchell's house. Piggy's uncle glares at Mitchell from that post.

"I just want to sit," said Piggy's uncle to Granny who appears puzzled since he made that u-turn back at the Methodist church.

Piggy's uncle is short in stature and has a funny voice like someone who just inhaled helium. This raspy tone is due mostly to too many World War Two cigarettes. He was so small that the Army Air Force once requested him to volunteer to be a tail gunner in a fighter bomber.

He was one of the few who could fit snugly into one of those glass cages at the back of the bombers. Piggy's uncle said, "nothing doing," however, to the Army Air Force and opted instead to be a cook for the infantry. That's where he learned his know-how to run a cafe on his own merit.

Old Man Mitchell notices him and stops his plowing. He looks at Piggy's uncle in a way that doesn't register anything on his face. Mitchell gives the reins a little snap to get his mule going again.

"There is goes plowing," said Piggy's uncle.

Some say Old Man Mitchell, who owned the "other cafe," burnt his place down for the insurance money because his cafe couldn't compete with the home style cooking of Granny's, especially her chili. Old Man Mitchell eventually admitted that he had left a coffee pot on the stove. It was this coffee pot that set off the great fire that nearly burned down half of downtown City of South Peeveetoe.

Nobody believed Mitchell much about not burning the cafe down for insurance purposes much though. Almost everyday he could be seen plowing in the hottest part of the day, his red hair and light skin reflecting burnt red and freckly in the brutal afternoon sun.

"It's like he's punishing himself for something," said Granny.

"I'm not the only one," said Piggy's uncle. "The whole town would have burnt down if not for Rachel's drugstore brick exterior."

"Saved us anyway," said Granny, showing several silver capped teeth as she tries to make light of it.

Piggy's uncle suddenly puts his head out the window and shouts, "Hey, I heard they found a rat in your chili once!"

Mitchell ignores him and plows with his head down. Piggy's uncle waits until Mitchell makes a ninety-degree turn with his mule at the end of the row. There the two glare at each other for what seemed like forever to the fidgeting Granny.

She finally can't stand the tension any longer and said, "I got to get back to snap some peas."

Piggy's uncle turns the key to start his green Studebaker and said to Granny, "I just hope he's ashamed of hisself!"

He sticks his head out the window before hitting the metal and yelled, "Well, I just got to say something!

CLAUDE WILKIES & HIS POOR WHITE FAMILY

C laude Wilkie's family, although white, are very poor. This is mostly due to his father being "a bad alcoholic." Once his father and his Army buddies drank rubbing alcohol and shave cream for want of it so badly. His inability to stop drinking, despite the fact that he had only half of his stomach left, led Claude's family to need government food assistance. Once a month they would pick up boxes in Beaumont filled with large white cans with nothing but "PEANUT BUTTER" written on the side of them, powdered milk, frozen fruit, or silver cans with a black drawing of a pig or a cow on the side.

The Wilkies moved far out to the country, nearly two miles out of town, near the old graveyard with the Civil War graves in order to save rent. They lived on armadillo and possum and hunted squirrel and deer out of season. They were so poor that all three kids would have to take a week off from school every year to pick black berries to sell to supplement their slaughter of wild hogs. Despite everything, all the boys in the Wilkies family were smart as whips and all of them made straight A's. The fact that they were good football players, even though they couldn't afford shoes and had to play barefoot, kept most from ridiculing them. Save that one bully with the bad teeth who went after Claude and his brothers with a bull whip on

Halloween and took their candy away from them.

One day, however, Claude got cornered by one of the pretty boy half backs in the bathroom of the old school, before they tore it down.

"Old Claude Wilkies is going to take a week off from school to pick black berries," said the pretty boy half back.

Claude laughs in an embarrassed way and keeps peeing with his back to him. Claude doesn't say anything back. He probably could have, as he knows the pretty boy half back in question has a father who blew his brains out with a shotgun. They say he killed himself because he couldn't afford to support his daughters in the custom that his neighbors could support their daughters. Claude is too proud to say anything back, even though he could have.

He feels someone standing directly behind him. Claude looks down to see a stream of yellow piss flowing directly underneath his own stream.

"If you move," said the pretty boy halfback, "I'll piss on your leg!"

Claude stays perfectly still. He doesn't want to get wee-wee'd on.

The big green door of the bathroom swings open and there is little Little Piggy sauntering in at the wrong time as per usual.

"Don't move Claude," shouted Piggy. "He'll piss on your leg!"

"I figured that one out Piggy," said Claude.

Claude doesn't move as the pretty boy half back slowly zips up his Lee jeans.

"See, I told you I wouldn't piss on you if you didn't

move," said the pretty boy half back. "Don't listen to Piggy Claude, his mommy won't even let him have a pellet rifle to shoot little birds with. Hell, he don't even have a four ten shot gun!"

"Maybe I don't have a four ten but I got a twenty two," said Piggy.

Stepping into Piggy's face, the pretty boy half back says, "Yeah, but your uncle don't let you use it except when he is there with you and that's only to shoot water moccasins with!"

The pretty boy half back stares silently then steps forward and punches Piggy hard on the arm. This knocks Piggy on to the toilet bowl where his hiney gets wet.

"You didn't say no pokes!" said the pretty boy half back.

Piggy grasps his arm and yells, "But I didn't cut one! You don't have to say no pokes if you didn't cut one!"

"It don't matter!" said the pretty boy half back as he pushes the door open to exit to his next class.

Piggy struggles to pull himself off the toilet seat but he is stuck. Tearfully, he yells, "Aw, you just jealous of Claude because you jealous of his adventurecomeness!"

SOUTH PEEVEETOE VIGNETTES

"Did you hear what happened to Elijah?" asks Bert.

"Elijah Fortunez?" says Fatty as he carefully squeaks a drop of oil from a metal oil can on to a ball bearing.

"They found him on his hands and knees in his house neked and barking like a dog."

"Then what'd they do?" asked Fatty, suddenly straightening up.

"Took him off to Rusk," Bert said. "He still there."

Fatty knew Rusk. It was the state psychiatric hospital located in the central part of the state. Old black Elijah had worked for Fatty at one time in the junk yard and was someone who was good a loading trailers with scrap metal.

"Poor old Elijah had nothing but trouble always his entire life," said Bert who suddenly felt sorry for him.

Elijah lived over in Nigger Town on the northeast side of South Peeveetoe, near the city dump before they ran them out and re-located them outside of town. Never that bright, he had only one arm due to an accident in the rice dryer and only one good eye. Even though he was over six feet three and strong as a bull, Elijah was afraid of just about everything.

"Remember when he got into that wasp nest?" said Fatty. "He was back working in that back field dismantling junk cars when out come the wasps. Turned out old Elijah was allergic to them and he took off like a shot. He ran like the lightning and waved his arms like he'd just seen a goblin."

Elijah's slowness of mind caused him to be the butt of every joke in the junk yard. Fatty would even, say, call his wife, "Aw Elijah," when she said or did something dumb.

"One day Elijah unscrewed the radiator cap while the engine was still hot and looked straight into it," said Bert. "It spewed straight up into his face. He screamed so bad we had to take him to the white doctor over in Greyville. Fortunately, under the circumstances, he agreed to see him."

"You say neked and barking like a dog?" asked Fatty.

"Wife left him," said Bert. "He had married that school teacher who had that boy that was supposed to be real smart. "She was always angry at him and called him, 'a black son-of-a-bitch,' all the time. That step child wouldn't have much to do with him. He looked down his nose at him. But they was all poor Elijah had. They was too good for him, however, and up and left him one day just like that. Elijah just couldn't take it anymore."

"And that's when they found him on his hands and knees alone in his house, neked, and barking like a dog?" asked Fatty.

"It was several days after his wife left before they found him," said Bert.

He and Fatty look off to the back field with the huge oak where Elijah had run from the wasps.

"Them old boys in the white suits had to take him off to Rusk," says Bert. "He's still there.

ITCHY

Itchy was too old to do so but once or twice a week he would make night raids on his bicycle and throw stink bombs or "secret messages" wrapped in handkerchiefs into his friends' yards. On these raids, he pretended to be Major Mosby and accented each stink bomb throw with a rebel yell before tearing off on his bicycle. Since he had failed twice, most of his friends were younger than him and were "used t'of him."

In two years Itchy planned to lie about his age, join the Marines, and play real army in Vietnam. Others tried to talk him out of it, citing Robert Reece who had gotten his face blown off there and was now like a zombie. Robert's cousin had been equally unfortunate and came back to South Peeveetoe in a box.

Cat Daddy Nugget went over there and got shot in the throat. He was different though as he was so loud that everyone was secretly glad he got shot so they could have some relief from his smart-ass ways.

Still, Itchy wouldn't listen. He couldn't hardly wait to go over there and play army for real. He could then return to South Peeveetoe with a blue silk jacket with "Seven Seas" written on the back of it. He could hardly wait to show them, "they was wrong about Itchy."

"Stop shaking the bed grand daddy," said Ray Junior.

"I'm not shaking the bed," said Ray Senior. "You're having hallucinating from the Scarlet Fever."

Weird diseases weren't so uncommon in South Peeveetoe. Mrs. Perkins had Rubella Measles and lost her new born baby. Several had polio as small children and never grew out of it. At least not in the right way. One was Ray Junior's sister who still had a steel brace that hooked up under her heavy, high-quarter shoes.

The most unusual case was probably a girl named Janine Leah who was absent from school for many months with Lockjaw. When she finally came back to school, somebody had to draw the straw to sit in front of her in the lunch room. Actually, there was really no choice at all as Mr. Gallazin made his class sit in alphabetical order, and, unlike the other classes, they were not allowed to talk.

As luck may have it, Piggy and Ray Junior both drew the straw to sit across from her. Ray Junior sat open mouthed as he watched Janine Leah try to eat her first school meal on her first day back. Try as she might, she could manage only a few sips of sweet milk through a straw. This, plus small forkfuls of pork and beans wedged between the teeth of a mouth that she could barely open.

Watching this painful act made Ray Junior weak and he asked Mr. Gallazin to excuse him early.

Piggy ate Ray's Junior's chili burger for him. He improved the flavor of it by sticking little potato sticks in it like they were candles on a birthday cake.

Sammy and Gerald were hanging out in the parking lot before school when Lonnie approached them.

"Y'all hear Jerry Swenson got run over," asked Lonnie.

"Do what?" asked Gerald.

"Last night, walking down the middle of the road, on Highway 70 between Greyville and Rice," said Lonnie.

"Doing what?" asked Sammy.

"Walking," said Lenny

"Where?" asked Gerald, spitting a glob of snuff juice at Lonnie's feet.

Lonnie dodges the dark brown snuff juice and said, "Home, I guess."

"Lost the only queer in South Peeveetoe," said Sammy. "Least the only one that cared to admit it."

Gerald snorts and said, "Cows, pigs, and sheep don't count."

Lonny spits tobacco juice, takes a swig of Coke, bites into a sandwich, and said, "He had to stop, since everyone made fun of him so bad, taking him to the drive-in movies and all. Weldon Young used to take him to the movies with him."

Sammy bit the top part of his lip and said, "Swenson went normal and began to act like a cowboy. He even wore a feather outside his cowboy hat in his brim just to fit in. It only made it worse."

"He had nothing but trouble his whole life," said Gerald. "I don't know if you know this, but he was my third cousin from my mama's side. Aside from, being a queer, you know, he was also an epileptic."

"Don't I know it," said Lonnie. "One night we was out drinking and he started having a fit and starting throwing up into the sink and shaking. We didn't know what to do, except watch."

"Who drove over him?" asked Sammy.

"Otis Rawlins," says Lonnie. "Going about ninety miles and hour when he hit him. Then he had to help the Highway Patrolman put him into plastic bag, Said it made him sick."

"And what did you get for Christmas?" asks Mrs. Traxler.

"A Barbie on a three-wheeler," says Louanna Louise, her eyes beaming.

Mrs. Traxler widens her eyes and holds her arms wide in exaggerated surprise.

She didn't normally sit for the family across the street from her as she was rich and they were poor. Mrs. Traxler made an exception this time as it was an emergency and she knew the lord her savior would want her to do so in his glory.

"They flew step grand daddy to the hospital in a helicopter," said Louanna Louise.

"I know that," said Mrs. Traxler.

"They say he's got gangrene and they are going to have to cut his leg off," said Louanna Louise.

"I know that," she said.

"Do you still teach school Mrs. Traxler?" asked Travis Wayne.

"No, I don't teach anymore," she said. "I stopped teaching when they integrated. They can't call me Mrs. Trailer House anymore."

"It was smart to get out then." said Travis Wayne.

"But you know it was never any of the coloreds children who gave me a hard time," said Mrs. Traxler. "It was always the so-called whites."

"We have a bunch of Mexicans living next to us," said Louanna Louise.

"I know there is, honey," she said. "They're the ones

with all the kids. They the ones who shell the oysters at their illegal jobs. And you know what? You have the prettiest blue eyes I have ever seen!"

Louanna Louise smiles with pride.

"And what did you get from Santa Claus, Travis Wayne?" asked Mrs. Traxler.

"Ah puppy," he said.

"A puppy?!" she asked in mock exaggeration. "Well, where is it?"

He looks at the ground and hacks the dirt with a pocket knife.

"It's dead," he said.

"Dead?" asked Mrs. Traxler. "Well, how did it die?"

"It got runned over," he said.

"The people next door to us runned over it," said Louanna Louise. "The ones with all them kids."

"You mean the Mexican man ran over it accidentally as he was backing up the drive way on his way to work one morning?" Mrs. Traxler asked.

"No," said Travis Wayne, who was named after his uncle.

"Did you see the puppy dead?" asked Mrs. Traxler.

Travis Wayne didn't answer but kept hacking the dirt with his knife.

"They took a club and beat it to death!" Travis Wayne said.

At that, little Louanna Louise whispered urgently to Mrs. Traxler, "he's making some of that part up."

Donald Lee's mother Nita smiles softly as she mops. Mrs. Gideon, the lady she cleans for, just a few minutes prior, confided to Nita that she had always thought Nita's only daughter was always the most beautiful baby she had ever seen. This compliment takes Nita back but it didn't keep her from puffing up with pride.

Still, she wondered to herself why Mrs. Gideon had never expressed this before. It had been years since her daughter was a baby. She was much older now and had already dropped out of high school and eloped with the Pentecostal preacher after the two were caught having carnal relations in one of the pews between services.

Nita pondered why people didn't tell other people the things they are thinking at the time they are thinking them. It also made her sad because for some reason it threw her back to thinking of little Prentice. Prentice was her second son from her first marriage when she lived over by the dump. He hadn't lived.

"I don't know if you remember Prentice," said Nita. "Nobody knew his real name. Everybody called him "Nigger" because he was so dark complected."

"Yes, I remember little Prentice, the one that died," said Mrs. Gideon.

"I'm surprised you, or anybody else for that matter, remembers," said Nita. She continues sweeping as she talks and said, "I blame myself for it. For not looking after him as well as I could have. He took sick one day out of nowhere. Doc Gibbons said it was due to the Whooping Cough."

Nita stops sweeping and gazes out the window of the kitchen and says sadly,

"You know, sometimes I look out the back porch screen door and I can just see little Prentice playing in the sandbox in the back yard just as clean as day."

If it is over five dollars you should lose your appetite.

Don't trust Yankees or women.

Buy things used. Recycle everything. Except cars which you should buy new as they will last but no automatic transmission, anything electronic, and no FM radio. Old things are better than new most of the time. They last longer. Do everything slow and thorough and you'll never have to re-do it again for thirty years. Don't fix things until you have to. Take in your own oil when you go in for an oil change. They don't mind.

Wear high tops for football shoes. They protect your ankles. Play on the line, not in the backfield. Guard, better than center. Center is the worst position. No basketball.

Wear a hat in the sun. Don't spend much on clothes, except for good work shoes. Always wear Mule Skinner gloves when you work and a long sleeved shirt, whether it is summer or not. Striped overalls are better than blue ones. Hot sun is just right. Work inside when it's cold.

Don't want anything. Don't need anything. But spend money on your hobbies such as season tickets to the Houston Oilers. And wipe your ass good.

No hunting until you're sixteen. No shotguns until then. No B.B. guns or pellet rifles. Don't kill birds. But you can shoot snakes with a .22. No Honda motorcycles. Cushman Eagles only. No Western Auto bicycles. Columbia only with big tires. No cats. Shoot them quick before they eat your birds in the trees.

Never pass up codfish in the cafeteria. Fried foods,

white sugar, OK. All right to eat the same thing for every meal. Round steak is just as good as the any other. Strawberry soda water, root beer, peanut brittle, peach ice cream, Mars bars are good. When you eat black-eyed peas, put a butter knife underneath the front of the plate so the pea juice will fall down to the bottom part of the plate so you can sop it up with light bread. Eat them with sliced fresh garden onions. Don't smoke them old cigarettes. Lights out early, up early. Whole family at meals. Be there on time or risk a beatin'.

Spread our your money. Put some in C.D.'s. Nothing wrong with sweepstakes either for that matter. You'll win eventually.

Collect bulldozers, tractors, and tools as they are hard to steal. Go to the Smithsonian someday but only for the Industrial Age Wing. And to the Ford Factory in Detroit. Avoid New York, save the American Indian Museum in Brooklyn. Read only history, mostly Word War Two and War Between the States. Picture shows used to be better than TV but now TV is better. Go to England at least once in your life.

Never use black with oil paints. Always mix Burnt Sienna with a little blue. Always gray your colors down. You can't buy good French drawing paper anymore. Or French brushes either. There are no good teachers of art anymore. Picasso ruined art.

Paint naked women on the side of your bomber in the war. Wash your buddies out of your bomber with a water hose. But never talk about your war experiences with anyone.

SOUTH PEEVEETOE DOG REQUIREMENTS

To be a South Peeveetoe dog you have to have certain characteristics and very high standards. You got to be brown, muddy brown is best, but you can have several other colors mixed in with that muddy brown. You must have lop ears, skinny, ugly and a pitiful looking multi-bred Heinz 57 type. If you are female you must have long tits hanging down because you just had puppies again. You also need to have a certain supply of gray, crusty mange and at least one blue tick, filled with blood to the brim, hanging off your ear.

You have to bark at anything. If you hear another dog barking, you have to bark at whatever they are barking at. It is mandatory to bay at the sound of the South Peeveetoe volunteer fire engine whenever it roars through town. In the day time you can either sleep under the house or sleep on the cool pavement of the Main street in downtown South Peeveetoe. You don't have to have enough sense to come out of the rain but you have to be able to get out of the way when a car comes honking down Main and needs you to move.

"How was your dinner at the trailer house with Judy Faye?" asked Lorrene.

"It was all right," said A.J.

"Well, what did she serve you in that trailer house of hers?" asked Lorrene.

"Oh, all the stuff left over from the Central Baptist congregation like creamed corn, chicken spaghetti, and a frozen cake. She likes to mix her spaghetti and meat and vegetables altogether."

"What did y'all talk about?" asked Lorrene.

"Mostly talked about people we knew back in school and where they are now and what they are doing," he said.

"Well, be careful," she said. "You can't believe everything she says. She twists things. Did she tell you she's been married four times?"

"No, she didn't mention that," A.J. said.

"See, she twists things," she said.

"There is one thing she told me that I kind of wondered about though," he said. "She said that the husband of a former classmate of ours came home one night and found her stuck to a Saint Bernard. He had to take her to the hospital to get the dog removed off her. Tell me, is that a true story?"

Lorrene blushes and wipes her avocado-colored-kitchen bar top with a dish rag and said, "Well, I am afraid that is sort of a true story. But it wasn't a Saint Bernard, it was a German Shepard. See, I told you she twists things!"

South Peeveetoe could be kind despite what everyone said. They don't send just somebody "to Rusk," the state psychiatric hospital in Rusk, Texas, just because they're different. Like the little old lady on the end of the road down by the community center. Everyday she walks to the post office looking for mail that is never going to show up.

Her only son had been sent to Korea and never came back. It was too much for her and she lost it as he was all she had in the world. Everyday from that moment on she would walk to the post office and check the mail for a letter from her son. Then she walks back home muttering to herself all the way.

One day Piggy and the mean preacher's kid were hanging out by the post office downtown when they saw her coming.

"There she comes." said the mean preacher's kid. "I will give you ten cents to listen to her and tell me what she is saying."

"Not enough Indian giver," said Piggy in a snotty tone. "I need enough for both a funny book and a piece of Bazooka bubble gum."

"All right, eleven cents," said the mean preacher's kid. "Just go ascertain what she is talking to herself about."

"OK," said Piggy. "Now what am I listening for again?"

"Find out what she is saying to herself," he said. "Are you flick-ted?"

"All right, all right," said Piggy.

Piggy goes over to the little brass and glass post office boxes, pretends he is opening the box next to the crazy lady, pauses, and then returns, acting as is whistling.

"Well, what was she saying?" asked the mean preacher's kid.

"I don't know, she stopped talking when I started listening," said Piggy.

"What did she say before she stopped talking?" he asked.

"She was mumbling something about her son fighting Hitler in Korea," Piggy said. "Now give me the Bazooka gum!"

One night there was a hard freeze in South Peeveetoe and the temperature went well below thirty, something it rarely did. The next morning, one of Fatty's men, Len Nard, a colored French if there ever was one, approached Fatty at the junk yard after he reported for work.

In a thick Cajun accent, Len Nard says, "Tell me Fatty, how the hell that engine block on my car going to break when I got that anti-freeze in my trunk, huh?"

Zig Zigafoose lives over in the house at the end of the street, next to the Little League field. He lives behind, not the Central, but the First Baptist Church. The one you see when you first come into town.

Zig Zigafoose makes his living as a television repairman. He lives there among a bunch of stray cats and dozens of black and white TV's stacked high on top of each other from floor to ceiling. When he is sober, Zig is known as an awful good TV repairman.

One day Fatty had a new idea, and, because of it, he decides to pay old Zig Zigafoose a visit and get his opinion on it. Fatty's sister-in-law bought what turned out to be the first color television set in the entire City of South Peeveetoe. She says she bought it so she could watch the Thanksgiving Day Parade each year in full color.

Fatty himself doesn't want one. He prefers the indoor picture show over in Trinity to TV but Mrs. Fatty was riding him hard about, "having one for the family." He decides to seek out old Zig Zigafoose for advice on the advisability of this decision. Fatty needs to have Zig check the vertical on his black and white anyway.

After Fatty knocks several times, Zig finally stumbles, bloodshot, to the door half awake.

"I got a black and white for you, and do you work on coloreds?" Fatty asked.

Zig grabs the black and white by the handle and said, "I wouldn't have a color TV and I'm not never going to work on them ever neither!"

He slams the door in Fatty's face. Fatty isn't angry though for he understands that a man must have his pride. When he gets home, Mrs. Fatty greets him at the door.

"Well, what did he say?" asks Mrs. Fatty.

"About what?" asks Fatty, pretending ignorance.

Mrs. Fatty sighed loudly and asks, "About the color TV?"

"Says he won't work on them and never will," he said.

Mrs. Fatty seems astounded by this and said in frustration, "Why, they're the coming thing! How's he going to live?"

"Run Piggy, run, they chasin' us." yelled Ree Ree.

"Where we running to?" yelled Little Piggy back.

"The man-made pond over by Charles Goode's home-made tree house!" said Ree Ree equally as loud.

Piggy and Ree Ree run for their lives as a herd of wild hogs bears down on them in the deep Piney Woods. They run for all they're worth for the pond, taking off their shirts as they go so they can dive in.

"I'm not going to make it!" shouted the gasping Piggy.

"You got to," said Ree Ree. "You know what happened to that Willenger boy! He fell off his horse into a group of them and they et him alive and them stomped him!"

Piggy takes off and speeds ahead of Ree Ree who they say is considered fast enough to run track on Junior Varsity someday.

Ree Ree looks back, sees the herd of wild hogs and their sharp yellow fangs, and yells, "They still after us!"

They make it to the edge of the pond. Before taking off their pants and shoes, both boys hesitate to look back to see where the wild hogs are located. The herd heads straight for them and Piggy screams.

At the last minute they part. Half of them head to the right of the boys and the other half go left. Then they see the real reason why the herd is chasing them. Behind the herd is Ree Ree's brother honking the horn on his Mo Ped and laughing his hiney off.

"Your oldest brother was making them chase us!" Piggy screamed.

"I'm going to go tell mama and she's going to beat you with the belt!" shouted Ree Ree at his brother with the long sideburns.

"You just mean and angry because your daddy fell off a derrick and left you the oldest," said Piggy. "I heard he reached for the derrick rail, and when there wasn't one, he fell and screamed all the way down, nearly two-hundred feet!"

Ree Ree's older brother, who had now started heading back to his house, slowly turns around when he hears Piggy's words. He brings the Mo Ped to a stop directly facing Piggy. Ree Ree's brother revs his engine by turning the handle bars and then does a wheelie and comes roaring straight at Piggy full-fledged with a sound louder than a lawn mower.

"Hey, my uncle will beat me if I get my pants wet!" shouted Little Piggy.

Ree Ree's brother was p.o.'d now, however, and doesn't stop. He comes right at him full speed ahead.

This time Piggy had to jump into the pond on his own, pants, tennis shoes, sleeveless shirt, and all.

Tommy LeVrier was born and raised in Daisetta, a tiny city in the Piney Woods region of Texas, just on the edge of Big Thicket National Park. Though the oilfield town is probably best known for the worldwide coverage received when it developed a sinkhole large enough to hold the Astrodome, Daisetta actually has long been fertile ground for artists. Besides Tommy, (son of painter Elbert G. LeVrier), it has produced Western author Bill Brett, Hall of Fame racecar writer Philip LeVrier, and actor Blue Deckert (Friday Night Lights TV show) among others.

LeVrier completed a Masters in Playwriting and Directing, at Texas State University. In cooperation with the University of Houston, playwrights Edward Albee and Lanford Wilson produced two of his plays at Stages Repertory Theater: Rapture Among the Oysters, and Phoebe. (It was the first time in 20 years a student was selected three years running for the Albee program.) Another achievement in this vein was being voted a finalist in the Motion Picture Academy administered Nicholl Fellowship in Screenwriting. The nomination was for his screenplay,

Running High and Looking Good.

Tommy, whose plays and stories have been described as akin to writing by Horton Foote, Sam Shepard, and Tennessee Williams, is a former news reporter and journalist. He spent four years at the Houston Chronicle, where among other journalism notices, he received the prestigious Lone Star Award.

Tommy's play, At Least He Didn't Die with Antlers on his Head! was produced Off-Broadway in 2013. Among the many testaments to Mr. LeVrier's writing, was a notice from Edward Albee, who found his work, "...provocative, often deeply disturbing, but leavened with a life-saving if dark sense of humor."

LeVrier's plays have been produced in Austin, Houston, San Marcos, Seattle, Los Angeles and New York.

CPSIA information can be obtained
at www.ICGtesting.com
Printed in the USA
LVHW090419081019
633405LV00009B/3914/P